TRANSFORMERS

Ultimate Storybook Collection

Little, Brown and Company

Hachette Book Group
237 Park Avenue, New York, NY 10017
Visit our website at lb-kids.com

Little, Brown and Company is a division of Hachette Book Group, Inc.
The Little, Brown name and logo are trademarks of Hachette Book Group, Inc.

The publisher is not responsible for websites (or their content) that are not owned by the publisher.

First Edition: April 2014

Sam's New Car and *Optimus Prime Versus Megatron* originally published in 2007 by HarperCollins Publishers
When Robots Attack! and *Operation Autobot* originally published in 2009 by HarperCollins Publishers
Autobots Versus Decepticons and *Bumblebee's Best Friend* originally published in 2011 by Little, Brown and Company
Prime Target originally published in 2011 by HarperCollins Publishers
Satellite Meltdown originally published in 2010 by HarperCollins Publishers

Library of Congress Control Number: 2013950455

ISBN 978-0-316-18865-4

10 9 8 7 6 5 4 3 2

SC

Printed in China

Licensed by:

TRANS FORMERS

Ultimate Storybook Collection

L B

LITTLE, BROWN AND COMPANY

New York   Boston

TRANSFORMERS

TRANS FORMERS

SAM'S NEW CAR

ADAPTED BY E. K. STEIN

ILLUSTRATED BY VAL STAPLES

BASED ON THE SCREENPLAY BY ROBERTO ORCI & ALEX KURTZMAN

FROM A STORY BY ROBERTO ORCI & ALEX KURTZMAN

AND JOHN ROGERS

Sam Witwicky wanted a car. Sam thought that if he had a car, kids might think he was cool. He worked hard in history class, and his teacher gave him an A minus. So Sam's dad agreed to help him pay for a car.

"Cars pick their drivers," said the salesman. "It's a mystical bond between man and machine." Sam looked at all the cars, but he kept spotting one in particular—a beat-up yellow Camaro with black stripes.

The salesman noticed Sam looking at the yellow car. "It's your lucky day," he said. "I'll give it to you for four thousand dollars."

Sam sat in the driver's seat and turned the key. He was so excited—he had his very own car!

That night, Sam woke up from a sound sleep. He heard his car roar to life outside. Looking out his window, he saw his car drive off down the street. "Hey!" he shouted. "That's my car!"

Sam knew what he had to do. As the car sped through the neighborhood, he chased after it on his bike. He had earned that car—he was not going to let anyone steal it.

Sam pedaled as fast as he could, and followed the car to the edge of town and up to a closed gate. The car smashed right through the gate and then stopped suddenly. Sam hid behind some crates to watch.

Fog hung in the air, making it hard to see, but for a moment it cleared. Sam could not believe his eyes. The car had changed shape! It seemed like it had arms and legs. Then a bright light beamed from its chest into the night sky.

Trembling, Sam turned around and met two guard dogs face-to-face. The dogs growled and snapped their teeth. With a yell, Sam started to run away.

The dogs bit at Sam, and he tripped. Suddenly, with a roar, the Camaro skidded to a stop in front of Sam and honked at the dogs. The strange form Sam saw in the fog had vanished—it was a car once again. It honked and drove in circles until the dogs were scared away.

Sam backed away from the car, not knowing what to do. Then, just as suddenly, the car was gone.

The next day, Sam saw the Camaro parked back in front of his house. He thought his car must be possessed. He called his friend Miles and told him, "It's alive! My car . . . it stole itself, it walked, now it's back! I'm coming over!"

Sam hopped on his bike to go see Miles. He looked over his shoulder and saw the Camaro following him. Sam pedaled faster, trying to escape the yellow car.

1

But there was no answer. Instead the car slammed forward, knocking Sam over. The headlights stretched out like snakes and circled Sam's face. Then the car transformed into a giant, sixteen-foot-tall, gray robot!

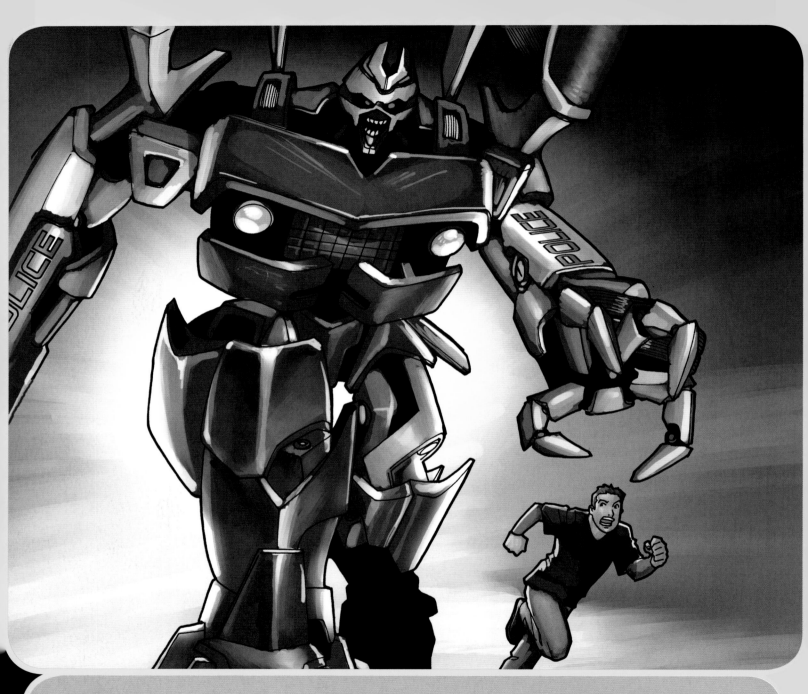

"This must be a bad dream," Sam said to himself. He was too scared to move.

"Have the Autobots seen the code?" the robot boomed.

"I have no idea what you're talking about!" cried Sam, who started to run.

The robot stomped after him and raised a gigantic fist. With a screech of tires, Sam's yellow Camaro appeared and crashed right into the gray robot, knocking him over. With the enemy down, the Camaro transformed into a yellow robot.

The gray robot rose and charged toward Sam. The yellow robot leaped in front to take the blow. He was knocked on his back from the force of the hit, but he quickly leaped up and grabbed a telephone pole, ripping it from the ground.

Using the pole as a baseball bat, the yellow robot swung at the gray robot and smashed him in the chest. Quickly transforming back into a Camaro, he popped open the door for Sam. As they drove off, Sam realized... his car just saved his life.

"Can you talk? What were you doing last night?" he asked the car. The car stereo turned on and flipped through stations.

A preacher on the radio called out, "A mighty voice will send a message, summoning forth visitors from heaven . . ."

"You were calling someone?" Sam asked. " 'Visitors from heaven?' Are you . . . an alien or something?"

Soon the car stopped on top of a hillside. Sam got out and stood beside him as he transformed back into a robot. Sam saw lights falling to the Earth. And, suddenly, his car was not the only robot in front of him.

Giant robots surrounded Sam. The largest one leaned down and said, "We are from the planet Cybertron. My name is Optimus Prime." Gesturing toward the yellow robot he added, "You've already met Bumblebee, guardian of Sam Witwicky."

"Bumblebee?" echoed Sam. In that moment, Sam knew he hadn't just found a new car—he'd found a new friend. An adventure awaited him.

TRANSFORMERS

OPTIMUS PRIME VERSUS MEGATRON

ADAPTED BY SADIE CHESTERFIELD

ILLUSTRATED BY VAL STAPLES

BASED ON THE SCREENPLAY BY ROBERTO ORCI & ALEX KURTZMAN

FROM A STORY BY ROBERTO ORCI & ALEX KURTZMAN

AND JOHN ROGERS

ot long ago on a planet called Cybertron, members of an alien race battled against each other. They were called the Transformers. Their war left the planet in ruin and forever divided two brothers.

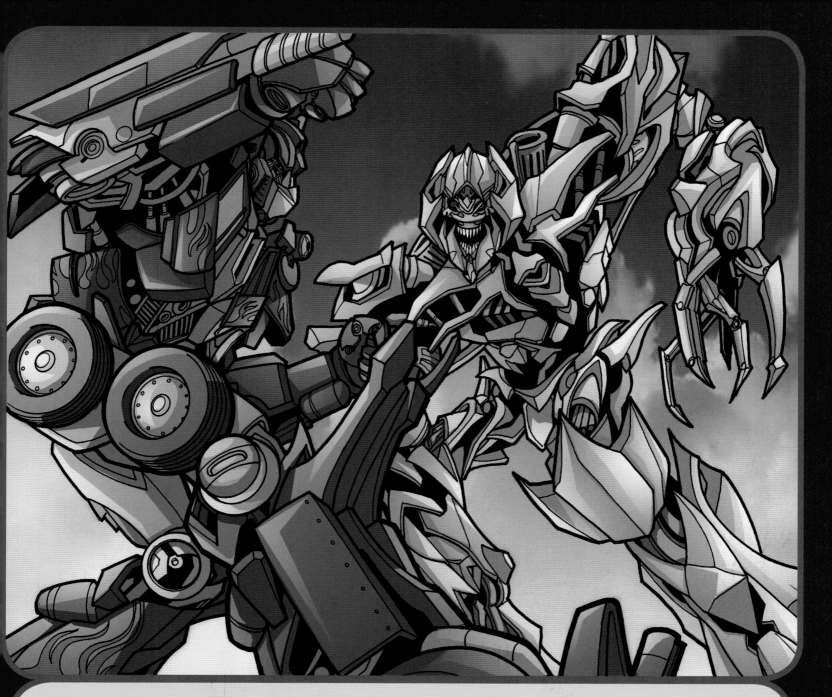

These brothers, known as Optimus Prime and Megatron, became fierce enemies. Megatron set out to conquer the planet. Because of this betrayal, Optimus was forced to battle his brother.

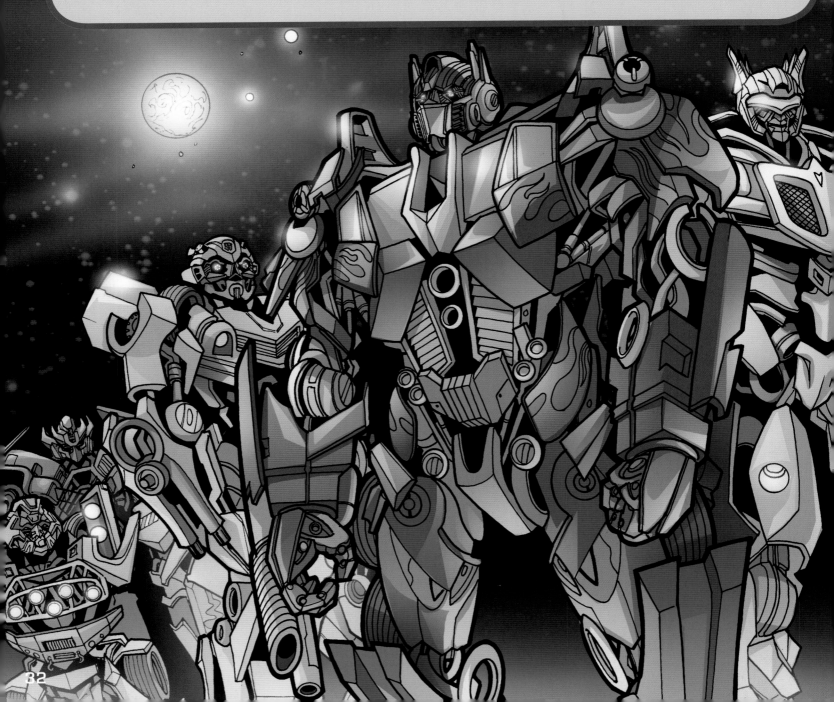

Optimus Prime led the Autobots, a group of Transformers who protected life in all forms. He was a wise leader, and quickly gained the respect of his army.

Megatron proved to be the opposite. He fed on the "Spark," or life force, of the defeated. He led his followers on brutal rampages. These Transformers were known as the Decepticons.

When the war on Cybertron ended, the Transformers who survived were forced to flee. Many came to Earth in search of the AllSpark, the supreme power that fills Transformers with the gift of the Spark.

The AllSpark could create new life for their ruined planet, and that's why the Autobots wanted it. The Decepticons had a different plan. They wanted to use the AllSpark's power to transform all of Earth's machines into an army with one single purpose: ruling the universe.

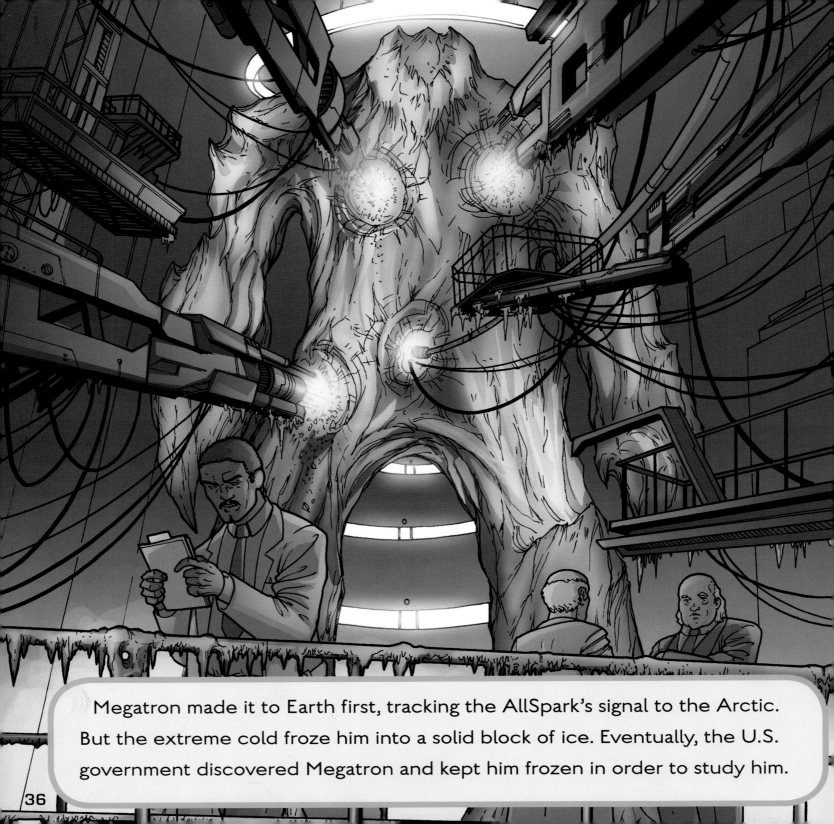

Megatron made it to Earth first, tracking the AllSpark's signal to the Arctic. But the extreme cold froze him into a solid block of ice. Eventually, the U.S. government discovered Megatron and kept him frozen in order to study him.

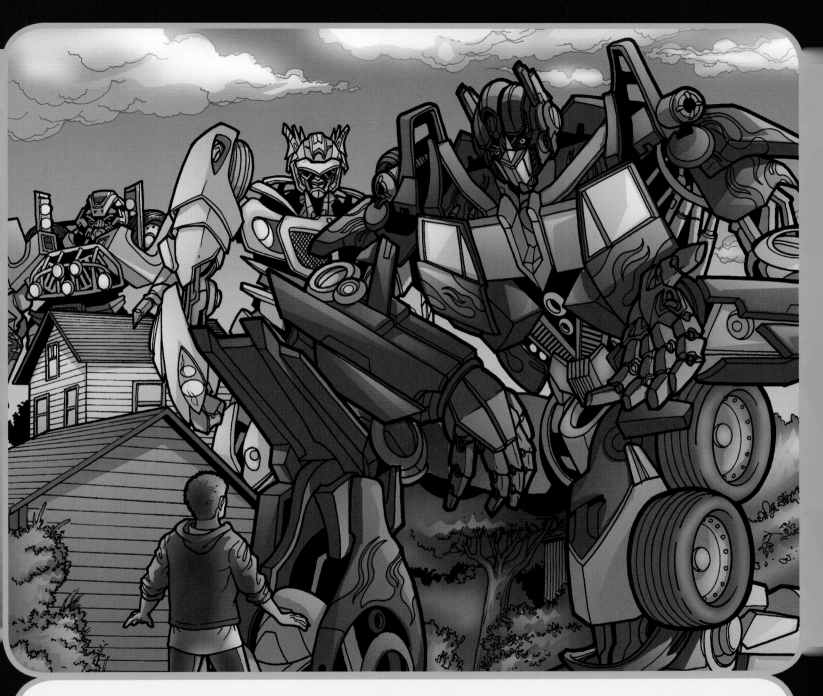

Optimus Prime led his army to Earth. He believed a boy named Sam had something the Autobots needed—an ancient code that revealed the location of the AllSpark. Optimus became friends with Sam and told him about the AllSpark.

Sam's great-great-grandfather's glasses had long ago been etched with the code. Optimus was able to read the code on the glasses.

"The AllSpark is two hundred and fifty miles from our position," he said.

An Autobot named Ratchet looked concerned.

"Prime . . . if we face Megatron, can you destroy your own brother?"

Optimus paused. "I will do what I must," he said, turning to his army. "Autobots, ROLL OUT!"

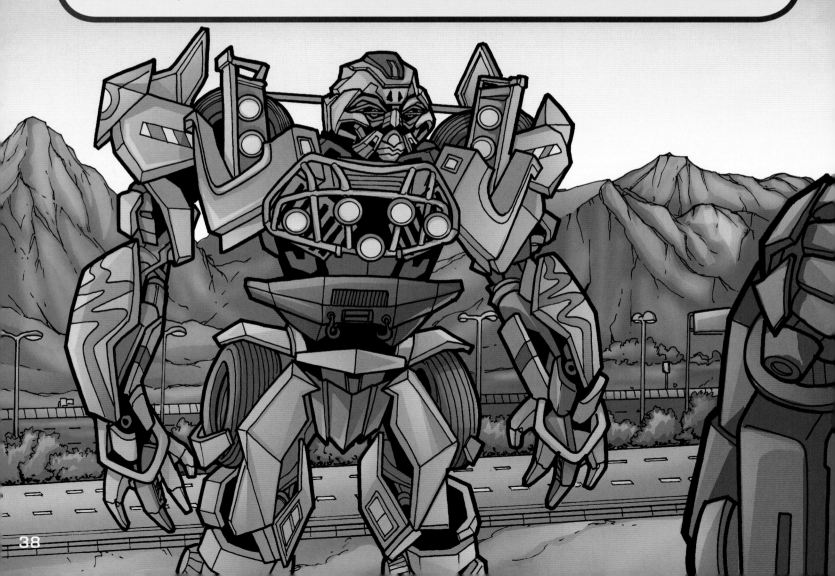

Under the Hoover Dam, Megatron was in a secret lab. He was still encased in a block of ice, just a few hundred feet away from what he wanted most: the AllSpark. Both were now the property of the U.S. government, but that was about to change.

Starscream, a fellow Decepticon, swooped down over the dam, blasting the power generator with missiles. Underground, the solid ice around Megatron began to melt. His eyes opened wide. The ice around him shattered with great force. He was free!

On a roadway near the dam, the Decepticons assembled for the return of their leader. They were ready to seize the AllSpark and conquer Earth. But the Autobots could not let that happen.

Arriving on the scene, they prepared to battle the Decepticons as they had on Cybertron. Then Megatron exploded out of the ground. He ripped out the Spark of an Autobot named Jazz. From a hundred feet away, Optimus Prime watched in horror.

Optimus ran toward Megatron, destroying everything in his path. Megatron tried to escape, but Optimus grabbed him, and the two brothers crashed to the ground. Megatron stared coldly at Optimus. "Brother, our war begins again . . . on Earth."

Metal fists flew through the air. Transformer fought Transformer. Sam looked on in amazement. He needed to help his new friends, the Autobots. In the chaos, he seized the AllSpark.

If he could get to higher ground, Sam might be able to escape on a helicopter.
Then the AllSpark, and Earth, would be safe from the Decepticons.

Suddenly, something exploded through the ground beneath him. It was Megatron! "Give me the AllSpark, boy! You aren't strong enough to defy me!" he yelled. Megatron fired at Sam, and Sam started to fall.

A giant hand grabbed Sam. It was Optimus! Sam was safe, but not for long. Starscream blasted Optimus, leaving him paralyzed. Sam was face-to-face with Megatron . . . and he was alone.

"Use the AllSpark, Sam! Aim for his Spark!" Optimus shouted.

Sam did just that. He jammed the AllSpark into Megatron's chest.

In a blinding flash, Megatron's Spark exploded.

It was all over.

With their leader gone, the last of the Decepticons fled the planet.

A few days later, Optimus watched as Megatron's body was lowered into the ocean.

"You left me no choice, brother," he said softly. The Autobots had won. The war was finally over . . . for now.

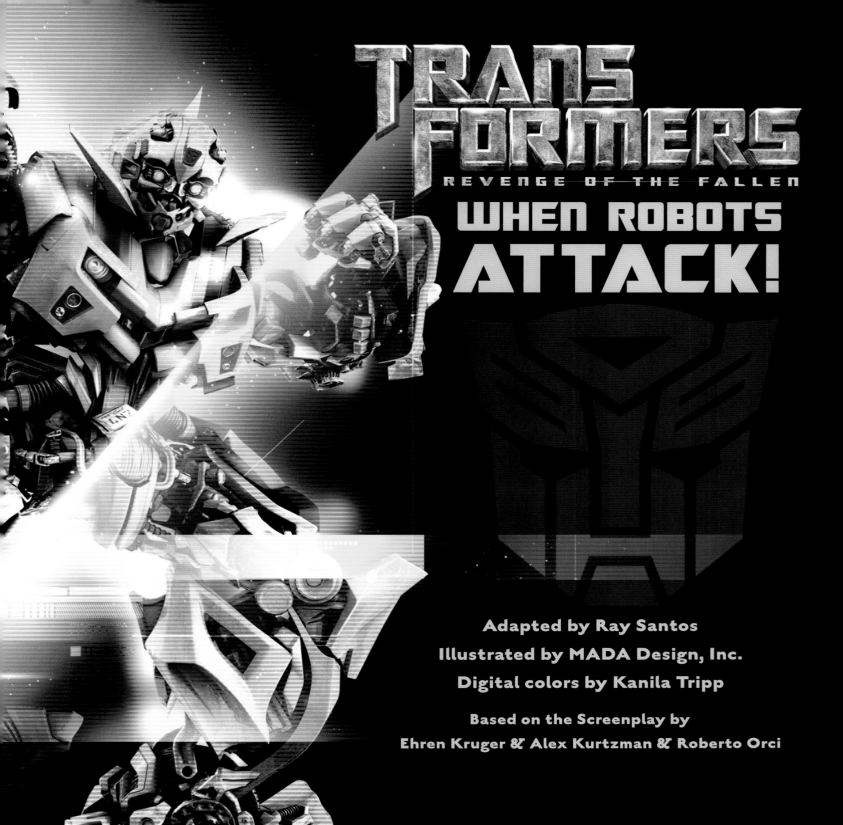

TRANS FORMERS
REVENGE OF THE FALLEN
WHEN ROBOTS ATTACK!

Adapted by Ray Santos

Illustrated by MADA Design, Inc.

Digital colors by Kanila Tripp

Based on the Screenplay by
Ehren Kruger & Alex Kurtzman & Roberto Orci

Two years ago, Sam Witwicky's life changed forever when his first car turned into a giant robot named Bumblebee. He was part of an alien race called Transformers, who had come to Earth looking for the AllSpark.

The AllSpark cube was the source of the alien life and could create Transformers from regular mechanical objects.

The evil Decepticons tried to use the AllSpark to rule the Earth, but Sam and his friends the Autobots fought back. Sam smashed the AllSpark into the Decepticon leader's chest, destroying both.

53

Things eventually returned to normal for Sam—if having a Transformer for a car was normal! Now Sam was packing for his next adventure: college.

"Look what I found!" said Sam's mom. "Your baby booties!"
"We're both real proud of you, kiddo," said his dad.
"You're the first Witwicky to go to college!"
Sam groaned and handed his dad a box to put in the car.

Up in his room, Sam sorted through a pile of clothes. He found the shirt he was wearing the day he had saved the world by destroying the AllSpark. Or at least he thought the AllSpark had been destroyed. When Sam held up the shirt, a tiny sliver fell out of the pocket!

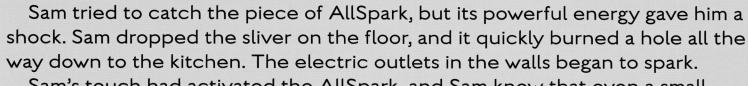

Sam tried to catch the piece of AllSpark, but its powerful energy gave him a shock. Sam dropped the sliver on the floor, and it quickly burned a hole all the way down to the kitchen. The electric outlets in the walls began to spark.

Sam's touch had activated the AllSpark, and Sam knew that even a small piece had enough power to create an army of evil robots. He had to destroy it!

In the kitchen, the AllSpark bounced off the counter with a burst of energy. Suddenly, all the appliances came to life. They were all changed into robots!

The cappuccino maker started shooting fireballs across the room. The garbage disposal used its sawlike blades to shred its way out of the metal sink. The microwave, electric mixer, and the blender all jerked to life!

59

In the kitchen, the blender noticed the water dripping down from the ceiling. Water could short out the small robots! The blender ordered the other Bots to march upstairs and find the source. The cappuccino maker left a trail of coffee on the floor.

Sam's dad came into the kitchen, but he didn't notice that all the appliances were gone. All he saw were the brown stains on the floor.

"Honey!" he called to Sam's mom. "I think the dog's started drinking cappuccino!"

In his room, Sam heard his dad's voice. *Oh, no!* He had to get his parents out of the house until he got the situation under control!

Sam tried to leave his room, but a tower of robots had already reached the doorknob . . . and they were coming in!

The appliances swarmed into the room. All of them had parts that had changed into horrible weapons. An egg beater hit Sam in the knees, and then the mixer started firing. Metal pellets hit the fish tank. Water splashed everywhere!

Sam hid behind his desk and looked around, but the only way to escape was through the window.

Sam climbed out of the window and tumbled to the ground. Luckily, there were some bushes to break his fall.

As Sam landed with a loud thud, his dad came out into the backyard.

"What's all the racket?" he yelled.

The electric mixer Bot looked out the bedroom window. Its arms turned into rocket launchers and started firing missiles.

"Dad! Take cover!" Sam called as the doghouse behind them exploded.

Sam's mom came running from the house with a waffle iron chasing her. "AAAAH!" she screamed. The evil robots were going to hurt his parents! Sam needed help.

"BUMBLEBEE!" yelled Sam. The yellow car with black racing stripes crashed through the wall of their garage and screeched to a stop in front of Sam.

The Camaro quickly changed into a giant robot.

69

The small home appliances were no match for Bumblebee. He was able to destroy the renegade robots with a few quick blasts from his plasma cannon.

The only problem was that Bumblebee also completely destroyed Sam's house!

Sam was relieved that the battle was over, but his mom was very upset. She turned to Bumblebee and yelled, "My house! I want that talking alien car out of here!"

Bumblebee knew that he was in trouble, but he didn't mind. He had done his job protecting Sam, and the family was safe again!

TRANS FORMERS
REVENGE OF THE FALLEN

OPERATION AUTOBOT

Adapted by Susan Korman

Illustrated by MADA Design, Inc.

Based on the Screenplay by

Ehren Kruger & Alex Kurtzman & Roberto Orci

Screech! Military vehicles squealed to a stop. A team of soldiers roped off an area for a top secret operation. They were tracking down dangerous aliens named Decepticons!

Soldiers leaped from the back of a pickup truck. The truck switched into the powerful Autobot Ironhide! Suddenly, the tracker blipped furiously. The enemies were close!

"Sideswipe, deploy!" commanded Ironhide.
A semitruck opened and Sideswipe, a silver Corvette, shot out. Sideswipe changed into a robot armed with swords.

The Twins arrived to help. "You just try to stay out of trouble, okay?" Ironhide told the mischievous robots.

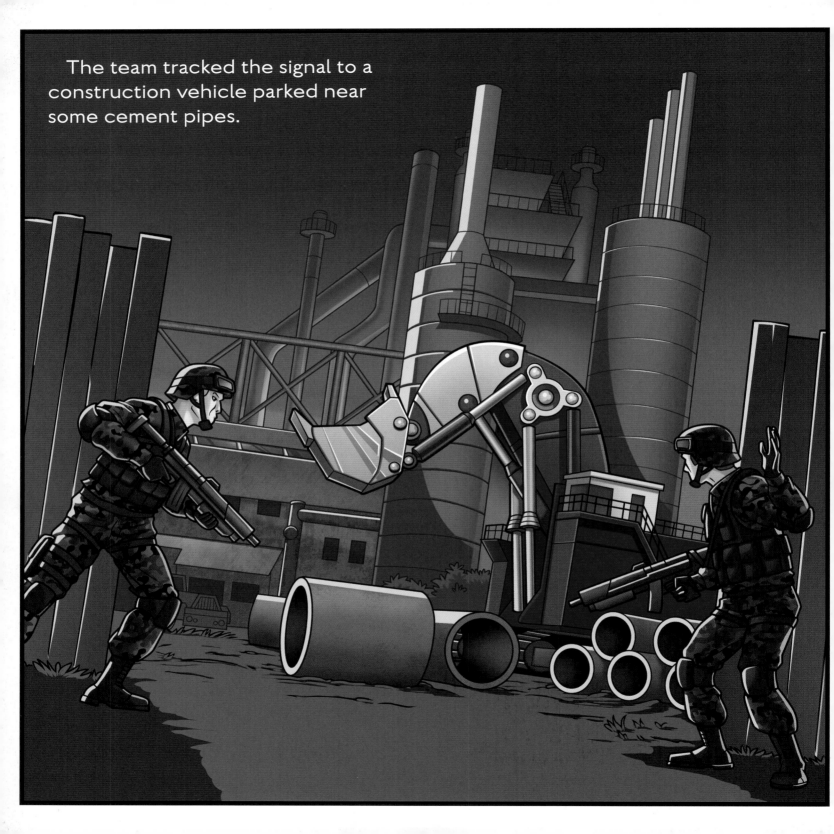

The team tracked the signal to a construction vehicle parked near some cement pipes.

Bam! The pipes were hurled aside as the machine changed into a giant Decepticon. It was Demolisher!

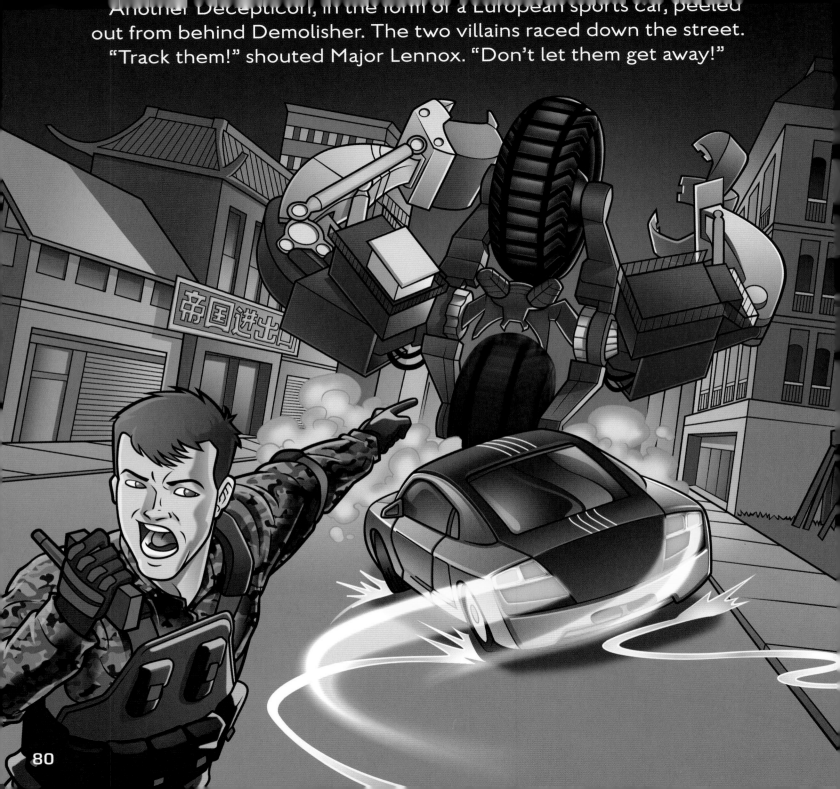

Another Decepticon, in the form of a European sports car, peeled out from behind Demolisher. The two villains raced down the street. "Track them!" shouted Major Lennox. "Don't let them get away!"

80

The Decepticon switched into his robot form, bursting through a brick wall!

The Autobots fired missiles at the enemy that shredded the sports car's steel skin, but the wounded Bot got back up.

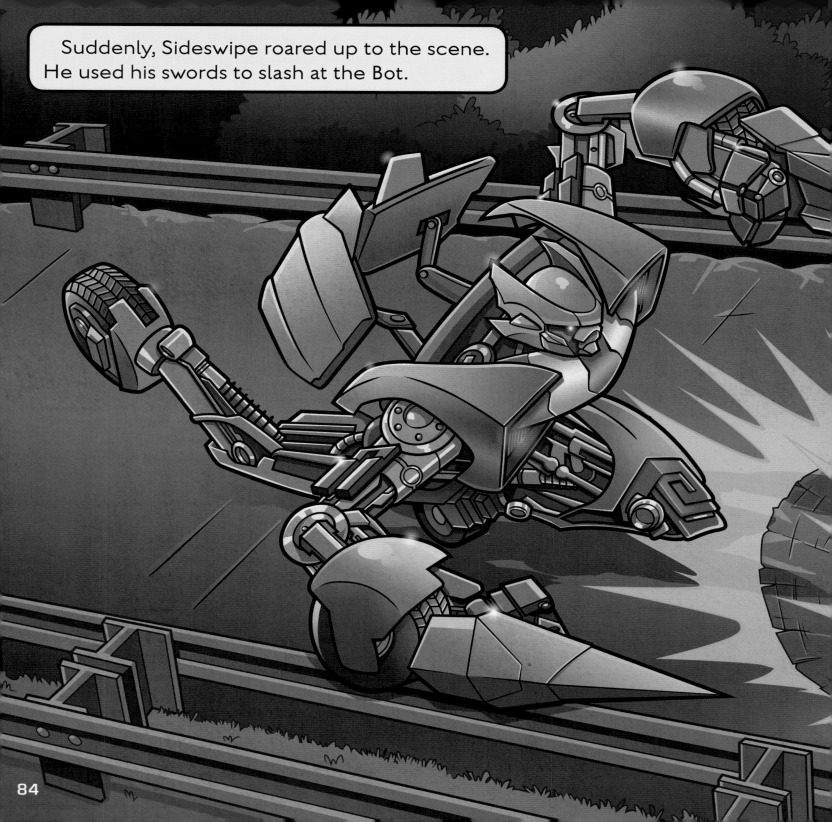

Suddenly, Sideswipe roared up to the scene. He used his swords to slash at the Bot.

The Decepticon fought back, sending a powerful energy pulse across the ground. The blast rippled down the street, rushing toward Sideswipe!

85

Sideswipe sprang out of the way just in time and advanced toward the Decepticon. With one swift motion, Sideswipe flipped the Decepticon's legs into the air, stopping it for good.

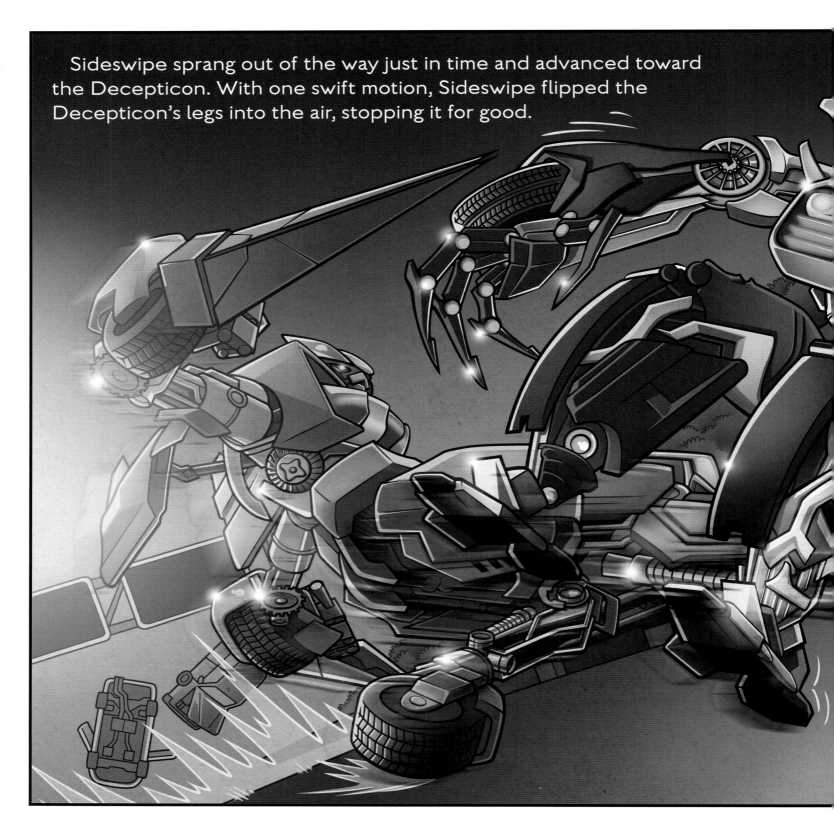

But Demolisher was still on the loose!
"Air support!" Major Lennox commanded.

A huge plane flew low over the city. The cargo hold opened to drop a semitruck. It was Optimus Prime—the commander of the Autobots!

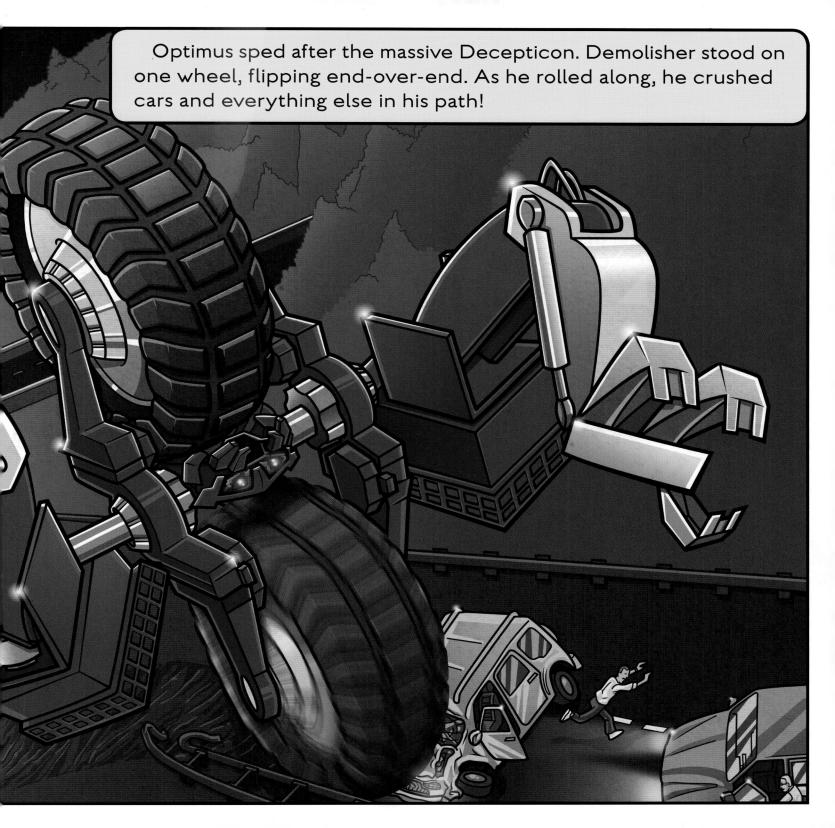

Optimus sped after the massive Decepticon. Demolisher stood on one wheel, flipping end-over-end. As he rolled along, he crushed cars and everything else in his path!

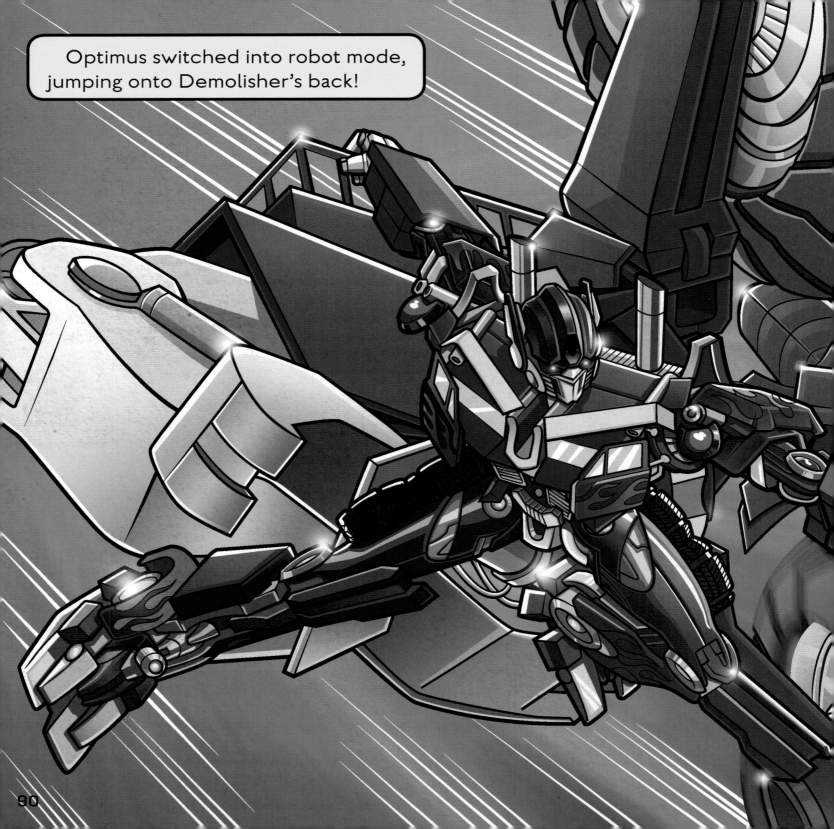

Optimus switched into robot mode, jumping onto Demolisher's back!

90

Meanwhile, Ironhide slid under Demolisher's giant frame and then swung onto one of his wheels. Together he and Optimus slammed into the Decepticon from both sides.

Finally, Demolisher wobbled to a halt. Optimus stood over his captured enemy. "Leave Earth alone," the Autobot ordered.

"This is not your planet to rule. . . ." Demolisher warned him, gasping for breath. "The Fallen shall rise again. . . ."

For now, the Autobots and their friends had stopped the savage Decepticons. But they knew they had to be ready. There was a bigger battle on the horizon.

TRANSFORMERS
DARK OF THE MOON

Autobots Versus Decepticons

Adapted by KATHARINE TURNER

Illustrated by MARCELO MATERE

Based on the Screenplay by EHREN KRUGER

Transformers have been living on Earth since fleeing Cybertron, their home planet, which had been destroyed by war. The Autobots have a peaceful agreement with the humans, but they know the Decepticons could attack at any time.

Optimus Prime is the leader of the Autobots. He arrived on Earth five years ago with Bumblebee, Ironhide, Sideswipe, and Ratchet. Since then, Wheeljack and Mirage have joined them to defend the people of Earth.

After a Transformers spaceship is discovered on the moon, Optimus thinks the Autobots have found another ally. The Autobot Sentinel Prime is Optimus Prime's old friend and had been stranded on the moon for decades.

Optimus Prime introduces Sentinel to his human friends.

Sam Witwicky has been a friend to the Autobots since they came to Earth, and he spends a lot of time with Bumblebee.

Colonel Lennox leads the NEST team, special soldiers who work with the Autobots to fight the Decepticons.

Sentinel explains to Sam and the NEST team that he had been on a secret mission for the Autobots when his spaceship crashed. He has secret technology—metal pillar devices that can open a Space Bridge.

"The bridge defies the laws of physics to transport matter through time and space," says Sentinel. "We could have used it to ship all the Autobots to a safe haven."

"You could have also shipped soldiers—or weapons," argues Lennox. Sentinel looks at Optimus. He is not used to small organic life-forms disagreeing with him. "These 'humans'…we call them allies?"

"We have fought as one, Sentinel. I would trust them with my life," says Optimus.

An alarm sounds throughout the base. The Decepticons are coming! "They want the pillars," says Sentinel Prime. "If they open a Space Bridge, it will mean the end of your world."

"Get all NEST forces back to base! We're under attack!" Lennox yells into his radio.

Optimus and several Autobots head outside to defend the building.

Ironhide and the NEST team scramble to form a protective ring around Sam and Sentinel. "Keep him guarded!" Sam yells. "He's the key!"

Sentinel looks at Sam. "Yes. As I always have been." Then Sentinel turns to fire a blast from his cannon at Ironhide. Sam cries out, "Sentinel, stop! What are you doing?"

"I am a Prime from the great planet Cybertron. I do not take orders from you!" Sentinel says with a sneer. The huge robot grabs the pillars and blasts a hole through the wall. He shifts into a fire truck and zooms out of the building to join the Decepticons.

107

The Autobots can't believe what has happened.

"Sentinel Prime is a traitor!" Lennox yells into his radio. "Alert the strike teams across the country now! Mobilize the Air Force!"

Sam and Lennox head out with the Autobots to search for the giant alien robot and stop him.

But it's too late. Sentinel Prime has already set up the Space Bridge near the Washington Monument! The pillars float in the sky, forming a ring, and a bright light glows in the middle.

The Autobots arrive on the scene.
    Optimus sees his old foe, Megatron, looking battle-scarred from their last encounter. But with Sentinel Prime at his side, Megatron knows he is stronger.

Far above Washington, D.C., on the dark side of the moon, thousands of Decepticons have been hiding for decades. They have been waiting for the Space Bridge to open. They can sense it is time. Five lights glow brighter than all the stars and then form a blinding white circle in the moon's sky. The Decepticons enter the portal, which will take them to Earth.

Behind Sentinel, thousands of Decepticon battle cruisers soar through the Space Bridge.

Watching with glee, Megatron cries, "Here we are! Fight us now!"

Optimus Prime looks at his former friend, Sentinel Prime, and asks, "Why?"

"On Cybertron, we were gods. And here...they call us machines," says Sentinel. "When only one world can survive, you would choose them over us?"

"Just over you," replies Optimus.

Optimus Prime, Bumblebee, Sam, Colonel Lennox, and their friends stand their ground as the Decepticons attack. This will be their biggest battle yet—but they are fighting for freedom and for the future of Earth.

It is their home.

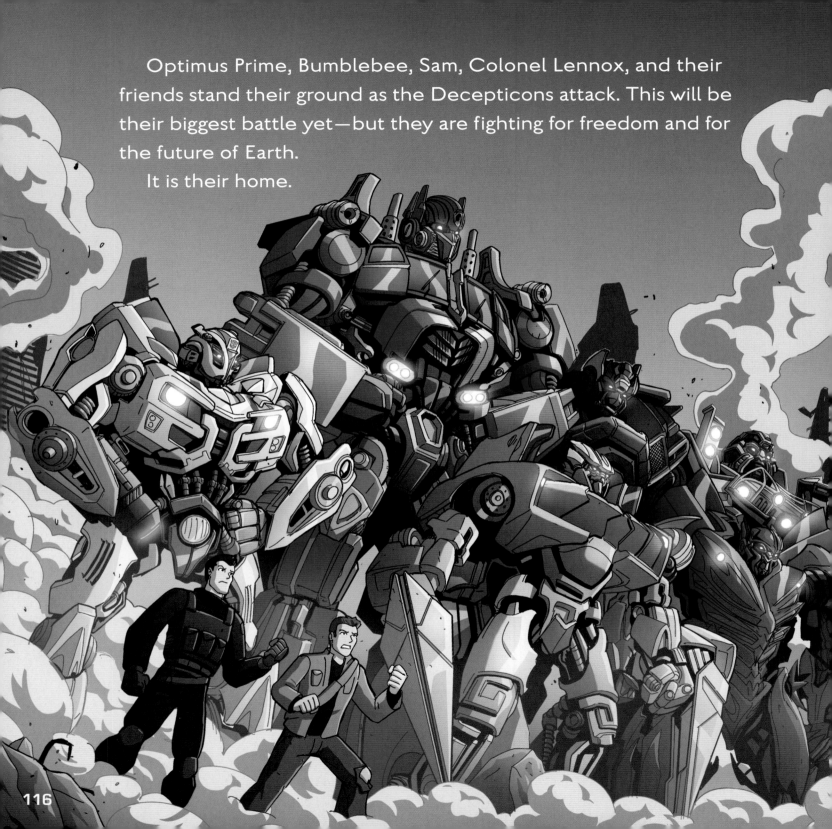

TRANSFORMERS

DARK OF THE MOON

Bumblebee's
Best Friend

Adapted by KATHARINE TURNER

Illustrated by MARCELO MATERE

Based on the Screenplay by EHREN KRUGER

Sam Witwicky saved the world. Twice.

He didn't do it alone. Sam's friends are the Autobots: alien robots called Transformers who live on Earth. Together, they have stopped the greedy Decepticons from taking over the planet.

Sam used to drive an awesome yellow and black Camaro that turned out to be a Transformer! The Camaro is really an Autobot named Bumblebee who became Sam's best friend.

They used to hang out all the time, but now Bumblebee goes on top secret missions—alone.

Sam has to drive a regular old car to his new job in the mail room at a big company. He misses his friend.

Sam delivers mail to everyone in the office. He wishes he had a cooler job. He defeated Megatron, leader of the Decepticons! He saved the life of Optimus Prime, leader of the Autobots! He and Bumblebee were a team!

Now he just hands envelopes to office workers. But today something strange happens. Jerry Wang hands Sam an envelope back.

"Mail boy!" whispers Jerry. "I know who you are!"

"Me?" Sam asks.

"Your robot friends are in danger," Jerry says. "The good ones. It's up to you." Then he hurries away.

Jerry must mean the Autobots! Sam thinks. He gets excited. His friends are in danger—but he can help! He'd better get this envelope to Optimus Prime right away!

But a computer on a desk next to Sam suddenly changes into a birdlike Transformer. It's a Decepticon spy named Laserbeak! He heard everything!

Laserbeak attacks. "Give me the envelope!" he shrieks between blasts.

Sam knows that the information inside the envelope is important. He has a mission now—and he won't fail!

Sam manages to escape and lock Laserbeak inside the office.

He hops into his car and races to find Bumblebee. Sam has to tell the Autobots that the Decepticons are back!

Inside the secret Autobot headquarters, Sam shows the envelope to Optimus Prime and the other Autobots. It contains top secret information about a Transformer found by Optimus and his team on the moon!

This new Autobot controls a powerful machine that the Decepticons could use to take over the world.

The next day, Bumblebee and Sam spend some time together. Sam decides to call his old friend Simmons to find out more about the Decepticons' plan. Simmons does some digging and calls back with alarming news: The Decepticons know about the new Autobot! They are on their way to steal the machine right now!

Bumblebee calls fellow Autobots Mirage and Sideswipe, and the three change into their vehicles. They must stop the Decepticons! Sam is at the wheel as Bumblebee, in his Camaro form, leads the pack. Sideswipe, as a silver car, and Mirage, as a red sports car, follow.

Suddenly, three black SUVs with flashing lights pull up behind the Autobots. "It must be the FBI, here to help!" says Sam.

But then the SUVs' tires squeal, and one of the vehicles shifts into robot form—it's a Decepticon! Long strings of metal chain hang from his head.

His name is Crankcase. He jumps onto Mirage's hood, facing backward. He raises an arm to smash the red car. He doesn't see the freeway sign until it's too late! *Smack!*

Sam hears Mirage's voice come over Bumblebee's radio. "Autobots, switch to Stealth Force mode!"

Sideswipe, Mirage, and Bumblebee alter their vehicle shapes to reveal supercharged engines and an array of cannons and laser blasters. "Awesome!" yells Sam. "Take out those Decepticons!"

With a squeal of tires and the smell of burning rubber, all three Autobots turn and open fire on the two SUVs.

One bad guy, named Crowbar, quickly turns to flee the scene. But Mirage and Sideswipe convert to robot form and chase after the enemy.

The last Decepticon, Hatchet, converts to robot form and charges directly at the Camaro.

"Uh, Bumblebee...?" Sam warns nervously as Hatchet rapidly approaches.

Bumblebee locks on his target and unleashes a barrage from his cannons. Hatchet is quickly defeated, and Bumblebee races forward to help his friends.

"I love this car!" Sam cheers.

Mirage and Sideswipe close in on Crowbar, with Bumblebee joining the pursuit. Outnumbered, Crowbar jumps up into the air and fires his missiles in all directions. Mirage and Sideswipe easily avoid the incoming rockets, and fire back.

But Bumblebee has to protect his friend! Before Sam knows what's happening, he is launched into the air. It feels like slow motion as he sees Bumblebee change into robot mode below. Bee does a crazy flip to dodge missiles before he catches Sam.

The Autobots have won!

Sam knows there are still more Decepticons to face, but he also knows that he and his best friend will help save the planet…again!

TRANS FORMERS

PRIME TARGET

Adapted by Susan Korman

Illustrated by MADA Design, Inc.

"I'll tell him!"
"No, *I'll* tell him!"
Optimus Prime finally interrupted the bickering twins.
"Please, somebody just tell me! Is Sam safe?"

140

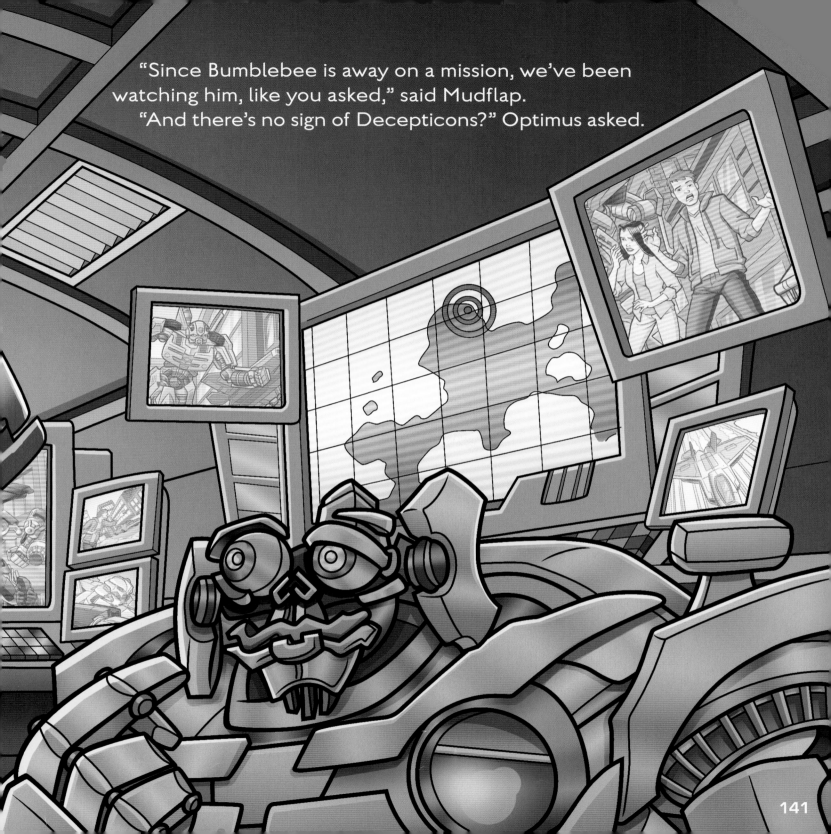

"Since Bumblebee is away on a mission, we've been watching him, like you asked," said Mudflap.
"And there's no sign of Decepticons?" Optimus asked.

141

The twins hesitated. "Well . . ."
"What is it?" asked Optimus.
"Sam is working on a supermagnet project in the science lab," said Skids. "There's a new research assistant—"

"And we think he's a Decepticon spy," Mudflap finished.
"Then keep your eyes on him!" Optimus ordered.
"And don't let Sam out of your sight either!"

Meanwhile Megatron, the Decepticons' leader, was plotting new ways to defeat the Autobots. "First I must destroy Optimus Prime," Megatron declared.

144

Then an idea came to Megatron. Optimus had a weak spot—it was the boy, Sam Witwicky! Megatron could use the boy to lure Optimus!

The new lab assistant *was* a Decepticon spy. Soon he was carrying out a special order from Megatron: Hack into Sam's computer and send a phony message to Optimus Prime!

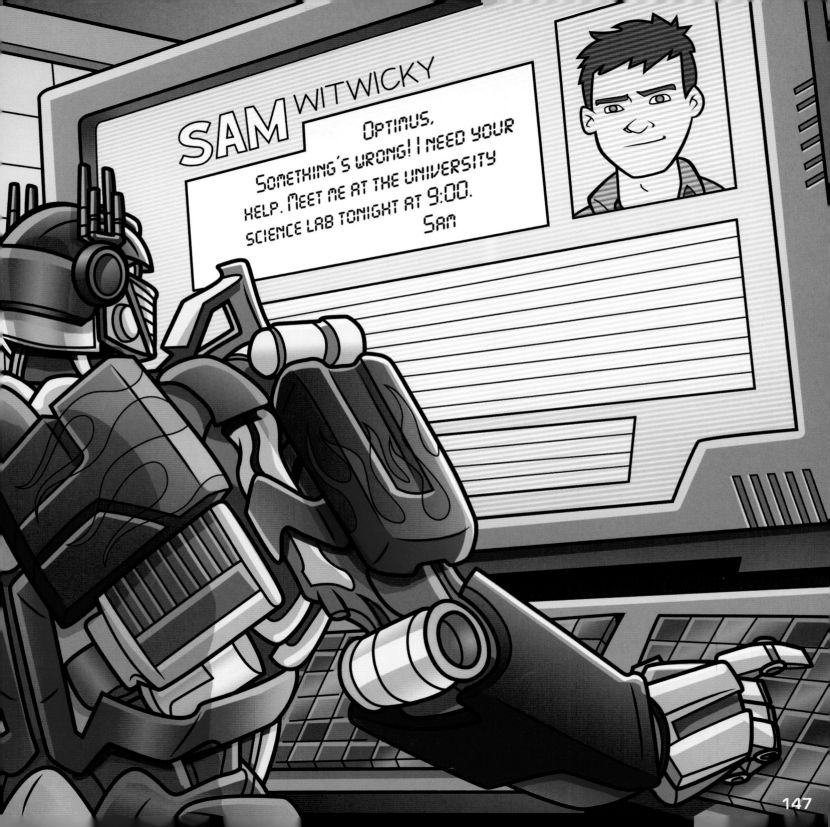

Optimus sped to the university to help Sam.

The science lab was pitch-black. When a light flickered inside,
Optimus caught sight of something. Megatron!

"Sam!" yelled Optimus. He revved his engine and crashed through the wall.

But as Optimus drove right into the building, he crossed the supermagnet's field. It pulled him in!

"Sam's not here!" Megatron gloated. "I tricked you, Optimus, and now I've got you just where I want you!"

Optimus furiously tried to free himself. But the supermagnet's force was too powerful.

Suddenly, Megatron flipped a switch, releasing Optimus. "Now I will destroy you!" the Decepticon bellowed.

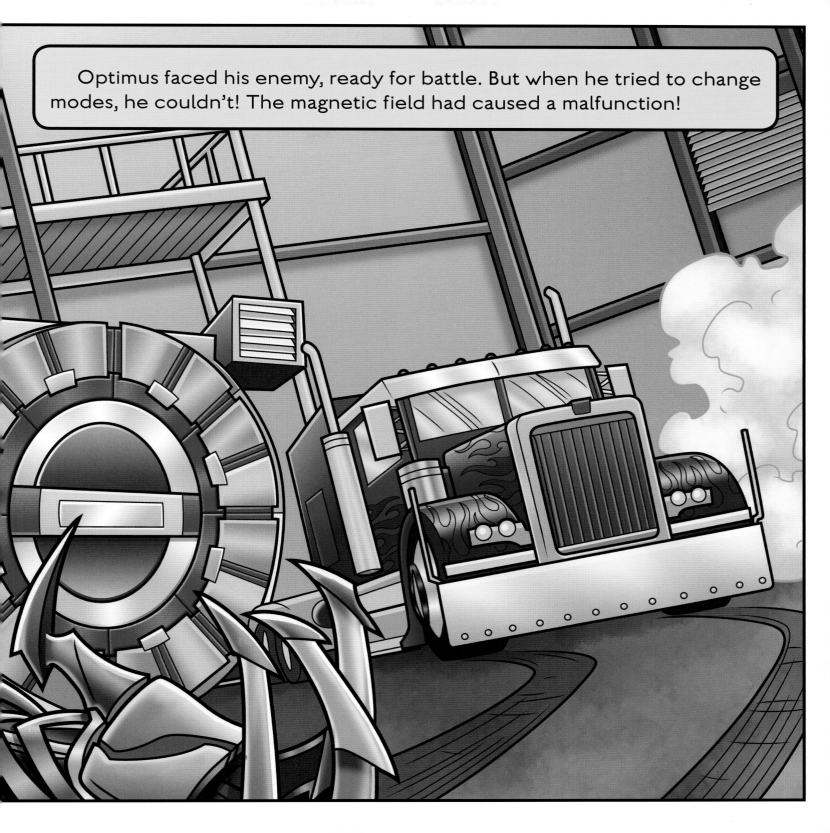

Megatron raised his massive claws and pounded Optimus again and again. Optimus shot into reverse, trying to get away. He spun, and then . . . *boom!*

Optimus slammed into a wall—and went completely still.

"At last!" Megatron cried. "I've stopped the mighty Optimus Prime!"

As Megatron stepped closer, Optimus suddenly blasted forward. He smashed into the Decepticon at full speed and sent him hurtling toward the supermagnet.

"Optimus!" someone shouted. It was Sam. "The Decepticons sent you a phony message!"

Sam ran into the lab and turned on the magnet. The machine whirred to life. Now Megatron was pinned there helplessly!

157

"Thanks, Sam!" Optimus signaled to Megatron.
"Oh . . ." said Sam with a grin. "I see you figured that out already!"
Just then more Decepticons roared up to the lab.

"Come on!" Optimus said. He wanted to get Sam out of there.
"Where are we going?" Sam asked.
"To find Ratchet," said Optimus. "I have to get my power back!"

"So can we stop spying on Sam now?" Skids asked Optimus. "You messed up Megatron's plot," Mudflap reminded him. "Sorry, twins." Optimus shook his head. "Our battle against the Decepticons is far from over."

TRANS FORMERS

SATELLITE MELTDOWN

Adapted by Lucy Rosen

Illustrated by Marcelo Matere

Deep in outer space, Soundwave grabbed a U.S. military satellite.

With his nimble metallic tentacles connected to the dish's signal, the Decepticon robot could hear everything that was happening on planet Earth.

Soundwave listened as his master, Megatron, battled Optimus Prime for total control over the planet. Megatron was a powerful, evil warrior with tricks to defeat even the strongest Autobot—but in this battle, he was no match for Optimus Prime.

"It's time for you and your Decepticon army to leave Earth for good!" Optimus ordered.

"I don't know how we could ever repay you," he heard the Autobots' human friend Sam Witwicky tell Optimus. "The Earth owes you everything it has."

"Your friendship is greater than any gift of thanks," Optimus replied. "That is all we really need."

"Those Autobots are always working together with humans. Their friendship is what's stopping us from tearing down that silly planet!" cried Soundwave.

Soundwave said, "I bet those Autobots wouldn't be so powerful if they didn't have the trust of their precious humans." He smirked as an evil plan started to take shape in his mind.

"Destroy, Buzzsaw and Ratbat!" Soundwave commanded as he sent his minions hurtling through the Earth's atmosphere.

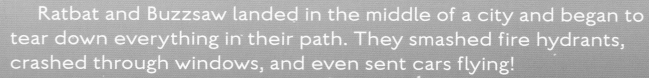

Ratbat and Buzzsaw landed in the middle of a city and began to tear down everything in their path. They smashed fire hydrants, crashed through windows, and even sent cars flying!

The police knew they had to act fast. "Call in Optimus Prime and the Autobots," they yelled into their two-way radios. "We're going to need their help!"

168

"Not so fast." Soundwave smirked as he listened in to the police call. Soundwave used his sharp tentacles to intercept the radio signal. He jumbled up the message the police were trying to send to the Autobots.

"Autobots, we have to roll out," Optimus said when he heard that there was trouble brewing. But instead of going to the city, where Ratbat and Buzzsaw were on a path of destruction, Soundwave sent the Autobots to an empty warehouse miles and miles away!

170

Soundwave sent a new signal over all of Earth's televisions, radios, and computers. "Your beloved Autobots have deserted you, humans!" he cried. "Surrender to the Decepticons or watch as your planet gets torn down, piece by piece!"

Sam Witwicky could not believe what he was seeing on his TV.

This can't be true, he thought to himself. *Optimus Prime would never betray his friends. Something must be wrong!*

Sam jumped into a bright yellow car with black stripes. "Bumblebee, let's go!" he shouted.

Sam's car was no ordinary Camaro. He was really an Autobot in disguise! Together Sam and Bumblebee zoomed off to find Optimus.

Over at the warehouse, Optimus and the Autobots realized that they had been tricked. "There's no one here," Optimus said. "Someone must have sent us the wrong message—it has to be Soundwave! No other Decepticon could scramble a signal like that."

Just then, Sam and Bumblebee pulled up.
"Optimus, hurry!" yelled Sam. "Ratbat and
Buzzsaw are destroying the whole city!"

Optimus and the Autobots wasted no time. They rolled into the city just as Ratbat was throwing motorcycle after motorcycle into buildings. Without thinking twice, Optimus grabbed the Decepticon robot by his wing and flung him as far as he could go—right into Buzzsaw!

The Autobots chased away the fleeing villains. "That takes care of that problem," said Optimus as everybody cheered. "Now to deal with the menace in outer space."

Optimus told his plan to the police. "We need the military's help. Send them a message—but not over a satellite signal!"

Soon, the military got Optimus's message. He asked them to blow up the satellite Soundwave was attached to! "Operation Satellite Meltdown is a go," they said.

The satellite exploded before Soundwave could get any word of what Optimus had planned. "Blast those Autobots!" he cried into the darkness.

Back on Earth, Optimus and Sam smiled at each other.
"Thank you for believing in us when it looked like we
had deserted you," Optimus told his friend.
"Your friendship is greater than any gift of thanks." Sam
laughed. "That's all Earth really needs!"

Read more TRANS FORMERS adventures!

TRANSFORMERS

PASSPORT TO READING **2**

Roll Out and Read Adventures

6 BOOKS IN 1!

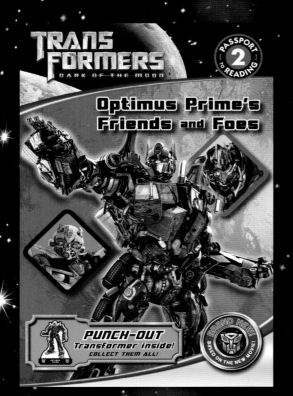

TRANSFORMERS
DARK OF THE MOON

PASSPORT TO READING **2**

Optimus Prime's Friends and Foes

PUNCH-OUT Transformer inside!
COLLECT THEM ALL!

BRAND NEW! BASED ON THE NEW MOVIE!

TRANSFORMERS
DARK OF THE MOON

PASSPORT TO READING **2**

The Lost Autobot

PUNCH-OUT Transformer inside!
COLLECT THEM ALL!

BRAND NEW! BASED ON THE NEW MOVIE!

TRANS FORMERS
P·R·I·M·E

TRANS FORMERS
PRIME
Meet Team Prime

PASSPORT TO READING 2

TRANS FORMERS
PRIME
Decepticon in Disguise

PASSPORT TO READING 2

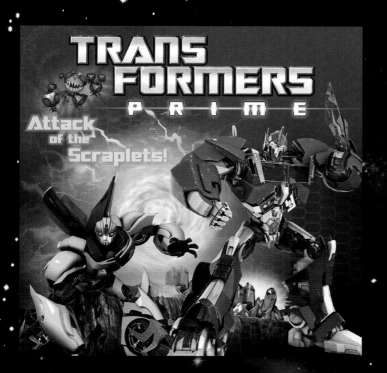

TRANS FORMERS PRIME

Attack of the Scraplets!

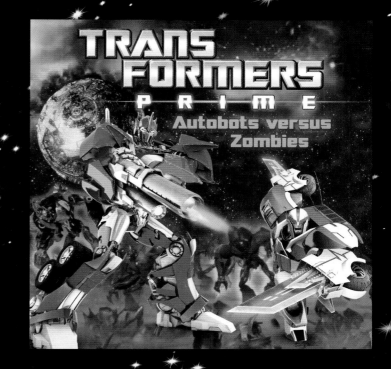

TRANS FORMERS PRIME

Autobots versus Zombies

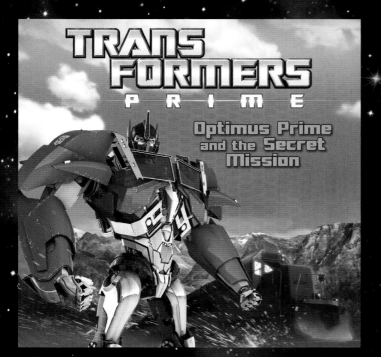

TRANS FORMERS PRIME

Optimus Prime and the Secret Mission

TRANSFORMERS PRIME

BEAST HUNTERS

Optimus Prime versus Predaking

TRANSFORMERS RESCUE BOTS

TRANSFORMERS RESCUE BOTS

The Mystery of the Pirate Bell

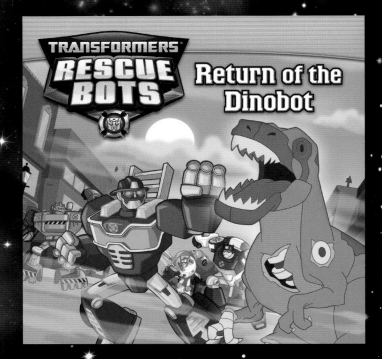

TRANSFORMERS RESCUE BOTS

Return of the Dinobot

TRANSFORMERS
RESCUE BOTS

PASSPORT TO READING 1

Meet
Chase the
Police-Bot

TRANSFORMERS
RESCUE BOTS

PASSPORT TO READING 1

Meet
Heatwave
the Fire-Bot

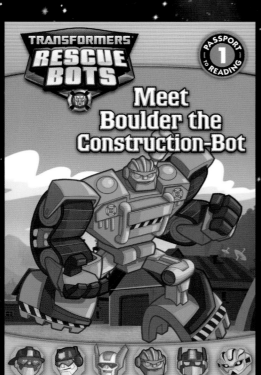

TRANSFORMERS
RESCUE BOTS

PASSPORT TO READING 1

Meet
Boulder the
Construction-Bot

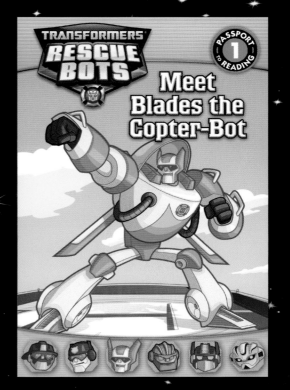

TRANSFORMERS
RESCUE BOTS

PASSPORT TO READING 1

Meet
Blades the
Copter-Bot

TRANS FORMERS

CLASSIFIED

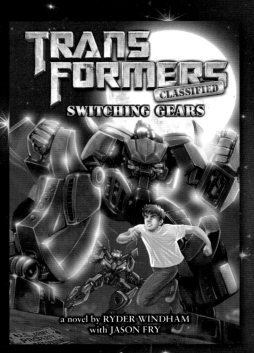

TRANS FORMERS
CLASSIFIED
SWITCHING GEARS

a novel by RYDER WINDHAM
with JASON FRY

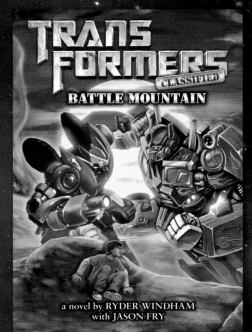

TRANS FORMERS
CLASSIFIED
BATTLE MOUNTAIN

a novel by RYDER WINDHAM
with JASON FRY

TRANS FORMERS
CLASSIFIED
SATELLITE OF DOOM

a novel by RYDER WINDHAM
and JASON FRY

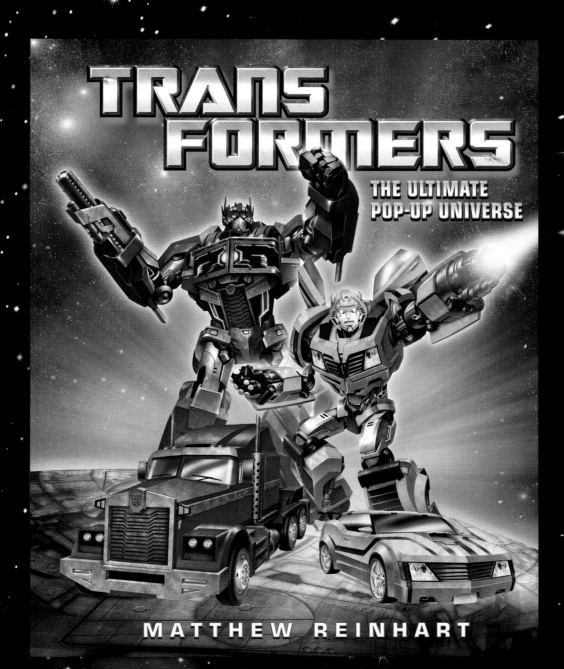

TRANS FORMERS

THE ULTIMATE POP-UP UNIVERSE

MATTHEW REINHART